This Book Belongs To:

_____

_____

*To Cole, Denver, Cassidy, Hudson, and Sydney - My five angels*

*To my husband Dan - Whose love and support has carried me through when I felt even one more step was impossible.*

*To my sister Kelly - I often find myself lost in memories of you, and such peace washes over me as I feel the warmth of your wings embracing me. Thank you for touching my life so deeply during the time you were here and for continuing to do so now.*

*To the brave soldiers . . . past, present, and future . . . Who risk their lives every day to protect our country. I stand in awe of your unselfish bravery and honor.*

*~ KS*

*To Liam and Brenna - All my love to you. . . never forget you are gifts to this world and you are cherished.*

*To Mom and Dad - Thank you both so much for always believing in me.*

*~ KJB*

There are moments in our lives when our world does not seem to make any sense. It is only time that brings clarity and purpose to situations that otherwise seem pointless and cruel.

Through compassion and a giving spirit, we can act as a lighthouse to others and help guide them through a raging storm to arrive at their purpose and destination much sooner, instilled with a fresh sense of hope . . . Knowing that even in the darkest of nights there are those who lovingly shine to guide us to a better place.

May "The Giving Jar" touch the hearts of all who turn it's pages. It is my sincere hope that this tradition finds a special place in your family now and for generations to come.

978-0-9824260-1-2
0-9824260-1-1
© 2009 Doodle Dots LLC

Printed in Hong Kong
www.doodledots.net

# The Giving Jar

## An inspiring discovery of humanity, hope, and the extraordinary power of love

Written by Krissy Smith

Illustrated by Katrina Jones Baden

www.thegivingjar.com

Upon Grandma's kitchen table sat an old glass jar. There was nothing fancy about it, just a simple glass jar. This jar never got to display the fresh flowers that I picked for Granny from her yard. Not once had it the pleasure of storing Grandma's sweet rhubarb blueberry jam. Instead, this jar sat empty on the kitchen table except for a worn piece of paper folded up into a sad little square. For years, I saw that same jar sit unchanged on Grandma's table.  One day, I decided enough was enough! I peered inside Grandma's pantry and spotted jars filled with all kinds of delicious fare. Jars holding golden apple butter, spicy dilly beans, and honey-packed peaches filled the dusty shelves. These jars had it made!  Even the jars holding the pickled eggplant had a better job than that jar that sat all alone on the kitchen table!

A rescue plan began to form in my head. I had a date that afternoon with an enormous trout that I had spotted on a previous fishing trip down at Big Gully Creek. I had just the right job in mind for that misused jar! My thoughts turned to visions of the jar happily teeming with slimy earthworms, crickets, grubs, and whatever other creepy crawlers I could uncover. This jar was in for such a treat!

I checked the kitchen carefully, twice for good measure, and saw that Grandma was busy rolling out dough for her apple-cinnamon pies.  This was the perfect opportunity to rescue this sad, sad jar. While Grandma hummed her usual tune off-key and the smell of cinnamon began to fill the air, I tiptoed over to the table so not to cause the wood from Granny's old floor to creak. I made it all the way to the jar without any disturbances.

My plan was perfect! Well almost perfect, and it would have worked, but I forgot to take into account one thing. You see, on the back of my grandma's head was an extra pair of eyes, and apparently these must not have needed glasses because she never seemed to miss a thing! She stood silently, studying my hands that clutched the jar. I tried quickly to think of an excuse, but it was pointless, guilt was painted all over my face.

I remained there awaiting my punishment when Grandma took a pitcher filled with her blackberry lemonade, two tall glasses, and headed out of the kitchen. I began to follow when Grandma turned and asked if I would please bring along the glass jar. I twirled around and retrieved the jar off the table, then raced to find Grandma.

When I found her, she was on the front porch sitting on her favorite wooden rocking chair with the green faded paint. Beside her on the table sat the glasses filled with her special blend that had made her a hometown celebrity. Granny gazed out into the beautiful summer day. The warm breeze tousled Grandma's hair and wisps of white danced across her wrinkled face. Droplets of water trickled down our icy beverages, making me aware of the bead of sweat that was starting to form on my brow. I was beginning to wonder if this was some sort of strange new discipline.

Grandma held out her hands and gestured for me to bring her the jar. Wordlessly, I crossed the porch and placed the jar that was causing me so much grief into her hands. She looked lovingly at the jar and placed her hand on the lid. Several years of sitting unopened and Grandma's unsteady grip was proving this jar rather difficult. After what felt like an eternity, she finally removed the cover. I was moments away from understanding the significance of this jar. Grandma tilted the jar in my direction and with her sweet smile, asked if I would remove its contents.

I took the jar in one hand and reached inside with the other. I carefully pulled out the brittle paper and looked to Grandma to see what I should do next. She responded by simply nodding her head as if to say continue. Very gently, I unfolded the note so as not to destroy this treasure that lay protected in the jar for all those years. The paper was discolored from age and the permanent creases added to its delicate state. I noticed that there was some sort of faint inscription scrawled on it. I took a moment to glance over at Grandma.  With her hands folded on her lap, she rocked slowly back and forth with her eyes closed.

My attention turned again to what I held in my hands. I had to narrow my eyes to try and make out the faded message. I moved over to where the sunlight was filtering onto the porch. With the extra illumination, I was finally able to decipher the writing.  It read,

"The Giving Jar - Always remember that you are surrounded by love, and with love anything is possible."

I held the paper in my hands for a few moments longer, trying to make sense of what it was that I had just read. These few simple lines scribbled on this ragged old paper were what Grandma had kept protected in the jar for all these years, as if she was some sort of pirate coveting her loot? Hmmmmm - That was it! There must be some sort of map on the paper or a hidden message leading to something marvelous! Like the Lost City of Atlantis or some 20-acre pond stocked full of 32-inch trout that would jump right into your hands, no poles necessary!

I unfolded the paper once again this time with much more excitement. Nothing! I turned that silly paper upside down, backwards, looked at it closely, examined it from a distance and not one thing different! If you were to ask me, storing slimy bugs would have made a much more interesting job for this jar.

I placed the note back into the jar and tried not to look too disappointed when I carried it back over to Grandma. She watched me with a knowing look as I crossed the porch, as if she realized I had no idea what to make of this whole thing. I placed the jar back into Grandma's hands, and she gestured for me to sit down beside her. We sat there for a few minutes without words. My thoughts began to drift back to Big Gully Creek and my trout when I was brought back to reality by the sound of Grandma's voice.

"You know, Billy, you remind me so much of your grandfather."  She bent over and softly kissed the top of my head. I noticed a single tear rolling down her cheek.  I was surprised to hear her mention Grandpa. Even though he had passed away long before I was born, it was still very hard for Grandma to talk about him. "When your daddy was just a wee little sprout barely even walking, there came a time your grandpa had to leave us. You see, everything that you and I have today, Billy, this house, the field where our pumpkins grow, and all the little things that make our life so wonderful, we have because of heroes like your grandpa."

Grandma paused for a moment as she took her handkerchief and dried her eyes. Hero - My grandpa was a hero? I thought to myself. All these years wondering and wanting to know about my grandfather, but I never dared to ask to spare my grandma the pain. I looked to Grandma, my mind racing with questions that had been waiting so long to be answered.  Before I had a chance to ask any questions, she continued.

"Your grandpa loved to fly. He used to tell me when he was soaring through the air, it was like dreaming with his eyes wide open. The only thing he loved more than flying was your daddy, me, and his country. So when Grandpa was called to protect

his country and his family, he could think of nothing more honorable or noble to do. I, on the other hand, was not so fearless. I pleaded with him not to go. Being the proper man that he was, he told me what I already knew, that his country was calling, and he needed to answer. He promised me he would return, that with the love that we shared it would take more than a war to keep him away from us for long. Every night I would rock your daddy to sleep in this very rocking chair and dream that tomorrow was going to be the day Grandpa would return to us. One bitter cold afternoon in January, I sat by the warmth of the fire rocking your daddy to sleep when I heard footsteps on the porch. My heart danced, the day your grandpa returned had finally come. I raced to the door with your dad in my arms and yanked the door open before he could even knock."

She paused just a moment, and I could see the pain on her face, as if she were reliving that day all over right at this very moment. "Standing before me was not your grandpa, but a gentleman dressed in the uniform of a military captain. I fell to my knees with disbelief. I knew what these visits meant. The captain told me how brave your grandpa was, how he single-handedly took down six enemy planes before the opposing side shot down his War Hawk. That because of him many soldiers still had their lives, and he was honored to have served beside such a fine man."

My eyes were fixed on Grandma, tears spilling down her face. I took a moment to process what I had just heard. I stared out into the lawn and watched the breeze sway the wooden swing tied to the branch of an old willow tree. I looked over to Grandma to find her tears had suddenly dried and been replaced with an air of peacefulness.

She picked the jar up she held on her lap and studied it for a few thoughtful moments before continuing. "Later that afternoon, a knock on the door came. News travels fast in a small town and I figured it must be a concerned neighbor checking in. I was not feeling up to company, but out of politeness I dragged myself to the door and opened it to discover that no one was there! I walked out onto the porch and found no trace of the mysterious visitor who had just knocked. As I headed back into the house, I noticed sitting to the left of the door was a jar."

Grandma glanced quickly at the jar in her hands then at me and continued. "I picked the jar up and took it back into the house with me. As soon as I was back in the warmth, I opened the jar, and inside it I discovered the jar's contents. The note was the very first thing that I had pulled out of the jar. I read it carefully, not really knowing what it meant, why this jar was delivered to my porch, or if this was even meant for me. The second item I retrieved from the jar was a small silver angel pin. I spent the next few minutes examining the tiny brooch. It was so beautiful, Billy, with one tiny imperfection. The tip of the left wing was slightly tarnished.

To this day, I cannot explain it, but as I pinned that angel on my sweater, a calming sensation washed over me leaving such a feeling of peace. I somehow knew this was a sign your grandfather was okay. That now he truly had wings of his own and could soar like an eagle."

I looked to Grandma and observed the angel that was pinned on her dress. It appeared to be shimmering with the tiny specs of sunlight bouncing off of it. I noticed the tip of the left wing seemed to be a different color than the brilliant silver that colored the rest of the angel. Grandma ran her fingers over her pin and in a soft voice spoke. "I have worn this angel faithfully every day since then. It makes me feel as if Grandpa is always close by."

"Was there a third thing in the jar, Grandma?" I asked letting my curiosity get the best of me.

A smile started to spread across Grandma's face as she happily replied. "The third thing I found in the jar was a bit puzzling. It was a golden bell, you know, the type that teachers keep on their desks."

"A bell, what in the world was a bell doing in the jar?" I wondered out loud.

"It took several weeks for me to understand what the meaning was behind the bell." Grandma paused just long enough to sip some of her lemonade and continued right where she left off. "I set the bell on a shelf and would glance at it several times a day trying to figure out its purpose. Then one day, it finally dawned on me! It was always a dream of mine to become a school teacher. I met your grandpa at a very young age, and we married soon after. I had no time for school nor was it something that we could afford. However, Grandpa knew that I had a desire to teach and promised that some day he would help make my dreams a reality. So, I decided this bell was a sign. I planned to go back to school when your daddy got a little older, and I did just that, Billy. It was difficult, many sleepless nights studying, but I never lost sight of my goal. Before I knew it, I was graduating and got my first job teaching in a second-grade class at Springcreek's Primary School. The bell sat on my very first desk in that second-grade classroom and every other desk I had thereafter."

She held the jar up once again and continued, "So you see, Billy, this jar that has sat alone on my kitchen table for all those years is a very important piece of my life. It helped me move through a very dark time, when all hope seemed lost, and brought me peace."

I suddenly felt guilty for ever wanting to take and fill this jar with anything, let alone something slimy! I gazed over at the jar and the note inside. Wow, all these years I thought this jar had a crummy job in comparison to the others in the house. Come to find out, it had the best job of all!

That afternoon, Grandma and I sat on the porch and talked for hours. As the sun moved across the sky and shades of pink and purple painted the horizon, Grandma told me stories about my grandpa, some of them serious some of them not so serious. My personal favorite was the story of how his nickname was "The Fly Man" with the neighborhood kids. When the children came around, Grandpa would pretend to catch a bug or fly and put it his mouth and eat it. He would make his act more authentic by finishing his routine with a big burp, which made him a huge hit with the kids!

What amazed me the most was just this morning I'd known very little about my grandpa, and here I sat this evening feeling like I had known him my whole life. I did feel some sadness that I never got to meet him in person. But it was quickly replaced with gratefulness for the memories I now had.

Soon the crickets began to sing their nighttime song, and hints of fireflies began to flicker in the air. Grandma rose from her rocking chair and told me she was turning in for the night. She placed a soft kiss on my cheek and took the jar with her as she went back into the house.

I wanted to stay outside and enjoy the summer night a little while longer. I sprawled out on the porch and watched as the stars appeared one by one. The day's events and stories of my grandpa rolled through my mind, and I slowly drifted off to sleep.

The morning sun filtered through the curtains and rays of light danced across my face. The scent of the gentle summer breeze mixed with the aroma of Grandma's flying blueberry flapjacks cooking on the griddle was

intoxicating. I stretched out from the tips of my fingers to the tops of my toes trying to recall how I made it from the porch floor last night to my cozy bed. My thoughts were interrupted by the rumbling of my stomach. I could not deny the bouquet of inviting smells coming from Granny's kitchen any longer. I rolled out of bed and scurried down the old wooden staircase and into the kitchen. Grandma was bustling around the stove flipping the golden flapjacks high into the air and tending to the bacon sizzling in the frying pan. I swear, there must be some sort of special classes out there just for grandmas because if I tried to do something like that, the fire department would be joining us for breakfast! I gave Grandma a peck on her cheek and wished her good morning as I darted to the cupboards to grab our table settings.

With my mouth watering from the sight of all the food, I ran to the table with my hands full and set it as fast as I could. As I was filling our glasses with the orange juice that Grandma had squeezed earlier that morning, I noticed the jar. It was right back where it always had been, as if it had never been moved. It was the perfect centerpiece for Grandma's table! Loving thoughts of my grandpa and the mysterious appearance of the jar flooded my thoughts leaving goose bumps on my arms.

I looked to the jar again. However, this time I noticed there was something sitting next it. Right next to Grandma's jar sat another that looked almost identical to hers. Yet, this one was empty. I couldn't imagine what the meaning

of this jar was, but I was positive it could not compare to Grandma's. Grandma crossed the kitchen with a platter full of our steaming breakfast and set it on the table. I wasted no time. I grabbed my fork and helped myself to a heaping stack of flapjacks and a mountain of bacon.

As I drizzled the warm maple syrup over my plate, Grandma began to speak. "I am so glad we had our talk yesterday, Billy! It made me realize that this jar has sat unused for far too long!" I sat listening to Grandma, my eyes fixed on her face while I stuffed forkfuls of flapjacks into my mouth. I watched her reach across the table and push the unfamiliar jar in my direction. I must have looked like a chipmunk with his cheeks stuffed full of acorns because Grandma couldn't stop chuckling at the sight of my flapjack-filled face and my eyes widening in confusion.

I wanted to ask her what the meaning of this new jar was, but according to Grandma, it was plain rude to speak when your mouth was full. Now regretting I'd taken such oversized bites, I chewed my food as quickly as possible, though before I could finish, Grandma had gotten over her giggling fit that left her unable to speak and went on.

"The time has come to share 'The Giving Jar' with others." I was anxious that somehow this would involve handing over our special jar to someone else. I began preparing my best defense on why this jar should never leave this kitchen table ever again. The thought of not seeing the jar sitting on Grandma's table left a sinking feeling in my stomach. My eyes drifted across the table and to my breakfast. Just moments ago I was famished, and now it had seemed I had completely lost my appetite. I glanced at the empty jar sitting next to me. I had practically forgotten all about that thing! I scooped the jar up off the table and enthusiastically glanced to Grandma for some sort of explanation.

In a split second, Grandma's gentle expression that she normally wore was changed to one of a boot camp drill sergeant. She looked intently into my eyes and with a powerful, stern voice, I had never heard Grandma use before, barked, "Attention, soldier!" Startled I sat there gaping at her, frozen to my chair with surprise and in fear that my grandma had gone mad! Throughout the years, she had been known for her crazy antics. For instance, for as long as I can remember, every year when one of us spotted the first robin of spring, we stopped what we were doing and no matter what the weather, we ran around the yard sporting pots on our heads and clanked pans together with old wooden spoons! Grandma said that our silly ritual ensured that we would have a long warm summer with just the right amount of rain for her scores of gardens to flourish. To tell you the truth, I don't think there was any reality behind it. Nevertheless, Grandma's gardens were always exquisite, from the plump ruby-red tomatoes to the sweet-smelling honeysuckle climbing up the front porch trellis. Not to mention it sure was entertaining to parade around like two wild baboons!

However, this sudden outburst of hers left me downright befuddled! She cleared her throat and positioned herself in a rigid military stance. At the corner of her mouth, a slight smile began to form. She quickly winked at me

easing my mind slightly, and then instantly resumed her straight-faced appearance. "Attention, Soldier." I sprang from my chair and stood up as straight as a board with my chest puffed out, head held high, and positioned my right hand at my forehead and saluted her.

Grandma's face was unchanging as she walked over to the table and retrieved the empty jar. She moved over to where a green canvas bag was lying and slid it across the floor until it reached the bottom of my feet. I was extremely interested in what lay hidden inside this bag. Every ounce of my being wanted to tear that sack open like a present on Christmas morning! It took all my strength to resist my curiosity and continue to stand at attention.

After all, my grandfather was a hero, and I reminded my grandma of him. Out of admiration for the kind of man my grandpa was, I had no other option but to show my strength of will. Grandma marched toward me with her elbows out and hands behind her back. She began to pace back and forth until she suddenly stopped midstride and shifted herself directly in front of me. Still holding the new jar in her hands she began to speak in military cadence.

"There is a top-secret mission that needs to be executed today by nineteen- hundred hours. This assignment will be riddled with excitement and danger and will require a great amount of stealth and skill." My pulse quickened with excitement at the news. Luckily I was able to maintain my outward appearance, but inside I was jumping with anticipation. My eyes were focused on Grandma while I struggled to keep the smile that was starting to form from completely overtaking my whole face. More than anything in the world, I wanted to prove that I was the right man for this job. If I lost my composure now, she would have doubts.

Amazingly, Grandma's form was not affected at all as she continued. "Pay close attention, soldier! This mission is of great importance and your focus is imperative to its success. 'Operation Giving Jar' has three separate phases, each of them of equal importance." I could hardly contain my enthusiasm. I was like a volcano on the verge of eruption. I wanted so badly to rush over to Grandma, wrap my arms around her, and thank her a million times over. Today, by far, was the most exciting day of my whole life. Fortunately for me, Grandma continued to speak, rescuing me from my own frenzied thoughts.

"Phase one. This step requires very careful consideration. For your very first task you will be expected to decide who the recipient of The Giving Jar will be. Do not be fooled by the simplicity of this phase. When you are making your selection, you must keep in mind that sometimes the ones who are in need of kindness the most are not always our favorite choice. I am confident that you will think very hard on this and will choose a person who is in need of their very own jar. Remember, soldier, a little ray of light even just the tiniest glimmer can cast away the darkest of shadows."

She hesitated just a moment, I guess for nothing more than to make sure I was paying attention and continued in her firm tone. "Phase two. You have already decided in the previous step who it is that is in need of the jar. Now what you need to decide is what should be placed inside the jar along with the note. You need to bear in mind that depending on whom you choose, the contents you select will be different. One person may be in the need of a bouquet of fragrant flowers to sweeten their day. For others it may be some fresh-baked cookies to soothe their tired soul. Human nature, soldier, it is a funny thing indeed. In a way, we are all connected. Everyone wants to feel loved yet our hearts are all different and unique. You must find something to place in the jar that will speak to that particular person's heart.

"Phase three. This is definitely the most dangerous part of the whole mission. You will need to deliver this jar to its final destination without being noticed by anyone. You cannot leave a trace of evidence to tie you to The Giving

Jar. You will come to find the rewards of doing things for others will not be found in the praise you may receive for your good deeds. The true prize is found within the joy you see on their faces and knowing that you have done something for someone else without the expectation of anything in return."

Grandma paused just a moment and looked at me and with the tenderness returning to her voice she continued. "The funny thing is, Billy, you will find doing thoughtful things for others is a lot like planting seeds. Special seeds of kindness will blossom into a bountiful harvest that you will enjoy for years to come."

I just stood there wordless trying to process all this information when Grandma moved closer and lay one hand on my shoulder and with the other brushed aside a piece of hair that had fallen out of place.

She moved her hand from my hair and placed it upon my cheek. With a soft voice she asked, "So, soldier, do you accept this mission?"

I took her hand that was placed on my cheek and held it tightly as I answered. "I am honored to be part of this mission." Grandma bent over and picked up the green canvas bag that was lying at my feet.

"If we are going to do this properly, you will be needing this," she said as she placed the bag in my hands.

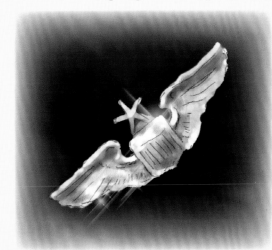

Without delay I unzipped the bag, and what I found inside left me speechless. Choking back the tears, I slipped into Grandpa's leather flyboy coat. I was only able to manage two simple words - "Thank you," I sighed as I breathed in the scent of old leather. The sleeves were a bit long and the leather was worn. Be that as it may, there wasn't a jacket anywhere that could even come close to measuring up to the one I was wearing now!

Grandma beamed with pride as she watched me examine every inch of my new coat. "Oh my goodness, Billy, I almost forgot!" Grandma exclaimed as she reached into her apron pocket. She pulled out something too small for me to recognize. "There," she said as she fastened whatever it was she had taken from her apron onto my jacket. "Now you are ready!"

Looking down to see what it was that she had attached to the coat, I discovered wings. "Grandpa's?" I whispered while my fingers swept across the pin that was positioned over my heart.

"Yes, Billy, This was your. . ." I darted across the room and threw my arms around Grandma, knocking the wind out of her and stopping her mid-sentence.

"Thank you! Thank you! Thank you!" I sobbed as I clung tightly to her. Grandma pulled away and took my face into her hands.

"You are welcome, Billy," she soothed as she brushed away the warm tears from my cheeks. Grandma slid the empty jar off the table. "There is much work to be done," she said with a smile as she placed the empty jar into my hands. "You better get started."

I rushed out of the kitchen with the unfilled jar to my favorite thinking spot. I positioned myself under the shade of the giant willow tree. While the sun rose high in the sky, the temperatures started to soar. With much hesitation, I removed my new coat and laid it in my lap while I considered the tasks that lay ahead of me. Recalling everything that Grandma had just said, I began to plan phase one - Who to give the jar to?

Many of my favorite people came to mind. First, there was my best friend Johnny. Filling the jar for him would be a cinch. Just off the top of my head, I already could think of at least a million things to put in there. Then thoughts

of my teacher Mrs. Steuernagel filled my head. She was so nice. I always imagined her with butterflies and other woodland creatures following her every where she went. Kind of like the princess in that story that Grandma used to tell me with the seven dwarfs.  Then there was Mr. Palumbo, the owner of Art's corner grocery store. He would always slip a few extra pieces of candy into my brown paper sack. My list continued to grow. However, there was something that Grandma had said earlier that kept echoing in my mind. "Sometimes the ones who are in need of kindness the most are not always our favorite choice."

Ugh, and here I thought this would be the easy part!  Everyone I was thinking of definitely deserved kind things done for them, but right now they all seemed so happy. I suppose happy people could always use a little extra kindness, but I just kept hearing Grandma's words.

Maybe there was someone out there who I didn't feel like deserved it as much, yet needed it more than those other people. Then it happened. Finally I had the name of the person who needed this jar more than anyone else I knew, old Mrs. Mulgrich.

Just the thought of her name made my toenails curl. She was a persnickety old lady who lived across the road from Grandma.  Instead of a smile and a friendly hello, she would greet you with a puckered-up brow and an unpleasant "Humph!" There had been rumors of her insatiable appetite for young children. I have never believed any of them. After all, I lived right across the street and she hadn't tried to eat me yet. The most terrible thing she had ever done to me was snatch up a baseball that had rolled onto her lawn all the while grumbling something about children having no respect these days. At long last, phase one was complete with Mrs. Mulgrich as my definite not-so-favorite choice.

I checked my watch. It was only noon or according to my new-found way of telling time, it was twelve-hundred hours. I was making excellent time, with only two phases left to go and about seven hours in which to complete them! I was feeling quite confident in myself for finishing the first task.

It seems my certainty was very short-lived, and it quickly vanished when the planning for phase two began. Choosing what to put inside The Giving Jar for Mrs. Mulgrich turned out to be more complicated than I had planned. Originally, I thought perhaps an old warty toad would be a very fitting pick.  Then again I was certain Grandma would not approve. Besides, I needed to choose something that would make her happy not frighten her! What was it that Mrs. Mulgrich needed? I thought to myself while I shifted under the tree to escape the searing rays that were trespassing on my shade.  Nothing was coming to mind. I couldn't even think of one thing. Clueless, on what to put in the jar, I remembered the note. This Giving Jar needed to have a note all its own.

With the jar and my new jacket in hand, I returned to the house to prepare the note.  I was hoping that while I was working on the letter I would figure out what else it was that the jar needed. I hurried through the kitchen, dashed up the staircase, and ran into my bedroom.  I quickly crossed the room to my desk and carefully draped Grandpa's coat over the back of my chair and situated Mrs. Mulgrich's jar on the desktop. I looked over all the different colors of paper piled in a neat stack and pulled out a crisp white sheet and selected a green crayon from my cup. After all, green was my favorite color and it is rather cheery!

I sat at my desk for a few minutes trying to recall the note that I had read just yesterday. At last, the words flowed back to my memory and I began to write,

"The Giving Jar -  Always remember that you are surrounded by love, and with love anything is possible."

I carefully studied over the words making sure no mistakes were made. Certain I had spelled everything correct, I folded the paper up into a neat square and slid it into the jar. I rocked back and forth in my chair as I shook the jar watching the note shuffle around the bottom. There was still that small problem that lay lurking in my mind refusing to be solved. What should I choose for Mrs. Mulgrich's jar? I remembered Grandma talking about picking an item that would speak love to her heart, or something like that.

I rocked in my chair thinking of different things that would make my heart feel loved like the Rebel Crickhopper Popper fishing lure that just came in at Baker's Bait and Tackle Shop. Or perhaps a tasty assortment of rock candy swizzle sticks. As appealing as these sounded to me they just did not seem like the right choice for Mrs. Mulgrich. Without a doubt, she was in some serious need of some cheering up. Something to turn her scowls into smiles. She must be very lonely over there in that big house all alone. She had no family that I knew of and she never had visitors. If someone were to even come close to her property, she would just angrily shoo them away. I glanced up at my calendar hanging on the wall above my desk and saw the 15th was circled in bright red. That was it!

I was going to make Mrs. Mulgrich a special invitation to the Springcreek's Annual Strawberry Shortcake Festival. Every year, Grandma and I went and I was positive I had never seen Mrs. Mulgrich there before. Maybe if she knew someone wanted her to be there, she would come and maybe if she came she could make some friends and not be so lonely and mean.

From my pile I selected a bright yellow sheet of paper and folded it in half, like a card, and began to draw. On the front, I drew a bright rainbow and underneath it a giant red strawberry. I chose a purple crayon, and with my very best handwriting I wrote, "YOU'RE INVITED!!!" I studied it over for a minute or two enjoying the vibrant colors and making sure I had all the colors of the rainbow in the correct order. After I was sure I was satisfied with the cover, I flipped it open and began working on the inside. I drew a bright yellow sunshine at the top of the paper, and all across the bottom I colored in green grass.

I drew in some flowers popping out of the grass, simply for the reason this invitation needed to be as cheerful as possible! With a crayon labeled "cadet blue" I drew a great big heart in the middle that spread across the whole paper and lightly colored it in. I stopped and admired my work for a few moments, pleased with how it was turning out.

I selected a red crayon and began to write inside the heart. Slowly, I spelled out "Dear Mrs. Mulgrich." I paused for just a moment to carefully choose the right words. I put my crayon back to the paper and began again.

You're specially invited to the

23rd Annual Springcreek's Strawberry Shortcake Festival!

When~ July 15th 1965 at 2:00PM

Where~ Whispering Willows Park

Space was running out on the inside so I flipped it over to the back and finished it off by spelling out "PLEASE COME!!!!" in oversized orange lettering. It was perfect! I could hardly wait to show Grandma The Giving Jar and what I had made to put inside it.

However, there was still much work to be done! Even now with the note and the invitation, the jar did not feel complete. As I was thinking, I opened Mrs. Mulgrich's card. When I saw the flowers peeking out of the grass, I realized what this jar was missing, a bouquet of fresh-picked flowers!

I rolled the card as if it were a scroll and gently slid it into the jar. When I released the card, it expanded and formed to the walls of the jar. I stood and pushed the desk chair in and grabbed Grandpa's coat.

Holding the coat, I gazed out my window, thinking about the sweltering heat. Even the birds that normally flittered about Grandma's many birdfeeders were taking refuge from the sun today, staying tucked inside their shaded nests with the occasional swoop down to the ground to pluck out an unsuspecting worm or two. It was decided, risking heat exhaustion seemed like a small price to pay for the honor of wearing this jacket.

I quickly slipped into Grandpa's coat, grabbed the jar off my desk, and ran down the stairs. Like a flash, I passed Grandma in the kitchen. With the door closing behind me, I called out to Grandma assuring her I would be back soon. I ran through the yard passing Grandma's many gardens. A variety of different smells rolling off the flowers and vegetables infused the air and combined to form one distinct scent. It was a comforting scent, one that made me think of Grandma. Soon the green grass ended and the field that held the most magnificent wildflowers began. As I crossed the threshold and entered the meadow, it felt as if I was stepping into a magical, wondrous realm. Butterflies danced cross the tops of the wildflowers, and the birds that dwelled in the nearby forest all seemed to join in and sing the sweetest melody that my ears had ever heard.

I stood captivated by the beauty of it all before the sun beating down on me brought me back to reality and the task at hand. I set the jar down carefully, noting where I had set it so not to forget. I wandered out further into the meadow and began to collect the rest of the contents for The Giving Jar. I started with a few brilliant orange daisies, added some black-eyed susans, and included a variety of other wildflowers that I did not know the names for. Each delicate flower was unique and it was almost magical to see how one tiny flower could transform the whole bouquet into something so magnificent. The colors of the flowers combined perfectly, reminding me of the rainbow on Mrs. Mulgrich's invitation.

With the bouquet complete, I ran back to where the jar was and checked my watch. Wow! It was 6 o'clock already! Where had today disappeared to? I had only one hour left to successfully complete this mission! I had The Giving Jar note, the invitation to the Strawberry Shortcake Festival, and now the bouquet of flowers. I still felt like the jar was missing something but time had run out. This would have to do. I grabbed the jar and sprinted back to Grandma's house as quick as I could without destroying the flowers.

Breathless, I entered the house and went directly to the kitchen. It seems that the planning of top-secret missions works up quite an appetite! Nevertheless, I did not have time to sit and enjoy the meal Grandma had prepared. Besides, I was too excited and hot to eat a full meal right now. After pleading with Grandma for a few minutes and promising that I would eat my supper as soon as the mission was complete, she agreed to just let me have a quick snack to hold me over. I am pretty sure it was my offer to eat a double portion of vegetables that finally persuaded her. I wish I would have known that the vegetable she had prepared for tonight's supper were lima beans. YUCK! I would have seriously rethought making that proposition. Oh well, it was too late now! Anyhow, I was too excited about the third phase of the mission to even worry about those disgusting lima beans.

Grandma had grabbed something out of the cupboard and with a tall glass of cold milk headed over to the table. I placed the jar down on the table and asked Grandma if I could have a container with water to place the flowers in. Grandma had barely set the milk down on the table when I scooped it up and began gulping it down. I was absolutely parched after my long afternoon. In all my 11 years, I never remember milk being so refreshing!

While I was drowning myself in milk, Grandma had placed Mrs. Mulgrich's flowers into a jar of water and set it next to her Giving Jar on the center of the table. She situated herself in a chair next to me and gave me a good looking over. Between her fits of laughter she managed to choke out, "Well, Billy, aren't you a sight to see!" I suppose I was, too. My face was as red as a beet, and while I sat slumped in my chair I rolled my empty glass, still ice cold, across my flushed cheeks in an attempt to cool myself down. My hands were in a serious need of a scrubbing from flower picking, and I noticed tiny burdocks that had hitched a ride on my pant legs. I must have picked them up from the field. They were probably trying to escape the heat!

"Yes, Grandma, I am a true sight to see!" I exclaimed as I walked over to the sink to give my hands a good washing. When I returned to the table, I noticed what it was that Grandma had taken out of the cupboard. "Cracker Jacks, my favorite!" I cried out while I tore the box open and began tossing the caramel-coated popcorn into my mouth. I checked my watch again to make sure not too much time had passed - quarter after six. Mrs. Mulgrich's house was practically right across the road, so I had time to enjoy a quick snack.

"So, soldier," Grandma whispered as if someone were going to overhear us "It looks like you have completed two out of the three phases. Do you care to share any of the details with your grand….Umm, I mean sergeant?" I had completely forgotten that Grandma had no idea how the first two phases unfolded or what my decisions were. While I munched on my Cracker Jacks, I explained to Grandma that I had chosen Mrs. Mulgrich. She had seemed quite pleased with my decision. That was until I told her I wanted to put a toad in the jar. However, I was able to regain her approval when I told her what I did choose! She thought it was a great idea to invite Mrs. Mulgrich to the festival and agreed that the flowers added just the right touch. Grandma left the table just for a moment and returned with some sprigs of baby's breath she had cut from her garden and a long piece of jute that dangled from her hand. She fussed with the flowers for a few minutes while I polished off the last of my Cracker Jacks.

I thought the flowers were just fine the way they were, but you know how grandmas can be. She strategically placed each flower in a certain position and added the baby's breath. She completed the arrangement by securing the flowers with the piece of jute and tied it into a bow so perfect only a grandma could have made it. I have to admit, the bouquet did look much prettier after she was done with it. I turned my empty Cracker Jack box upside down and shook it to make sure I did not miss any pieces of popcorn hiding in the corners trying to escape their fate.

Something fell out the box and landed with a clink and rolled across the table. The tiny trinket spun on its side for a few moments and landed right next to Mrs. Mulgrich's jar. I could not believe my good fortune! My prize from the Cracker Jack box was the missing piece that was needed to complete The Giving Jar. Lying next to the jar was a silver ring with some sort of flower design on the front. I picked it up to examine it closer and found the back of the ring was not closed; it could be adjusted to different sizes!

Grandma watched me curiously as I dropped the ring into The Giving Jar. I explained to her that adding the ring was an obvious choice. It was just Mrs. Mulgrich's size and from what I could tell, most ladies loved jewelry. Grandma agreed with my decision and said she would be delighted to receive such a fine gift. I checked my watch again - 6:30 on the dot. Phase three was about to begin.

I stood and brushed the popcorn crumbs off my pants and straightened out my new coat as I zipped it up. I gathered up the jar and the flowers and looked to Grandma. "Permission to be excused?" I asked with a smile.

"Permission granted, soldier!" Grandma replied, smiling. As I turned to walk away from the table, Grandma called out, "One final thing before you go." I turned and waited for my orders. Grandma stood from her chair and brushed her fingers across Grandpa's wings that she had fastened on my jacket earlier.

"You are a fine young man, Billy. I am very proud of you and Henry. . . I mean your grandfather, would be very proud of you, too." She laid a gentle kiss atop my head and softly said, "I love you." Before I could even return the sentiment, Grandma quickly followed with an, "As you were soldier." and gestured to the door. I turned to rush out the door, but before I left the house I had one last thing that needed to be done. I called out to Grandma and echoed back the words the she had just said to me. "I love you." and with those final three words, phase three began.

I stepped out onto the porch thankful the heat had finally let up some. There were even traces of a refreshing breeze, which was a welcome change from the stagnant air from earlier in the day. I stared across the yard at Mrs. Mulgrich's house and began to devise my plan. Today was Thursday so I was sure Mrs. Mulgrich would be home. She never left her house except on Tuesdays to go grocery shopping. We did have other neighbors who lived on our road, but luckily our houses were too far apart for them to notice me, even if they were outside. So it seemed very simple. All I would need to do is cross the road, put the jar on her doorstep, knock, and run out of sight before she opened the door.

"Tink! Tink ! Tink!" The jar in my hands was starting to shake causing the ring to hit the glass. I suppose jars can't shake themselves. So I'll have to admit that it was my hands that were trembling. I know this is going to sound preposterous, but what if she actually did eat children? What if the moment I stepped on her porch she had a booby trap set up and she caught me? Then after she had me, she'd cook me up with some cabbage and carrots and turn me into some sort of Billy stew! Pull yourself together, man! You are a hero, remember, and if that means facing some child-eating, fastidious old woman, then so be it! Time to check my watch – 6:45. . . I prayed a silent prayer and set off to complete the final phase of my covert mission.

I ran through Grandma's front yard, careful not to drop the jar or damage the flowers Grandma had so care-fully arranged. When I made it to the road, I could see into Mrs. Mulgrich's lawn and had a clear view of her front porch. It did not appear that she was outside, and from what I could tell she was not on her porch either. Even though there are very few cars that travel down our road, I checked to make sure nothing was coming. As I suspected, the coast was clear.

There was no turning back now. I ran full speed ahead right into Mrs. Mulgrich's yard. It turns out trying to run with your hands full while spinning your head side to side to make sure you aren't being spotted is not as easy as it sounds. I must have overlooked the gopher hole in the middle of the yard. Before I knew what had happened, the tip of my sneaker got caught in it and I was sprawled across Mrs. Mulgrich's yard! This was definitely not part of the plan! Nevertheless, I had a mission to complete, and it still could end in success. The good news was, I had not been spotted. I hadn't broken any bones, and somehow I managed to keep the jar and the flowers from becoming a casualty of my clumsiness. I collected myself, checked my watch - 6:47- and continued.

Within a few seconds, I was up the stairs and standing on Mrs. Mulgrich's front porch, so far so good. I hadn't fallen through any trap doors into a cauldron of boiling water or been swallowed up by a net and strung to her porch ceiling. There was a window on the porch that I would have to cross in order to reach her door. I did not want to risk getting caught, so I lay down on my belly and took turns sliding the jar and flowers and pulling myself forward with my elbows. After what seemed like an eternity, I finally made it to the door. I was so thankful not to have been spot-ted in this compromising position. How would I have explained that one? Good evening, Mrs. Mulgrich. I am just out trying to earn my Boy Scout badge for good deeds. Tonight I am cleaning off my neighbors porches by slithering across them on my belly. Something tells me that would not have ended so well! While I was still lying down, I placed the flowers into the jar and positioned it so it would not tip over when the door was opened. I got onto my feet but still stayed crouched down low to stay out of view from the window. I quickly knocked three times.

"YELP! YELP! YELP!" Oh, no! How could I have forgotten Mrs. Mulgrich had a dog? Actually, it was just a tiny little ankle biter, but man, did that thing have lungs! It didn't bark like any other dog that I had ever known. Instead, it shrieked a high-pitched blood curdling, Yelp! Now, because I was distracted a moment too long, I had no time to run. I heard footsteps coming toward the door and some mumblings about what kind of person would knock on the door at this time in the evening. There was more, but I couldn't hear it all because while she was walking toward the door, I jumped her porch railing and landed in the bushes. Fortunately for me, I was able to get under one of the bushes just enough to hopefully not be discovered.

I held my breath when Mrs. Mulgrich opened the door and bellowed out a stern "Hello." She said a few more things but I could not hear them over the yipping of her hyper little alarm system. I thought for sure that pooch was going to be the death of me. But luckily the next thing I heard was, "Come now, Truffles. Mummy doesn't want you catching a cold." Thankfully, the little noise box listened and turned and ran directly into the house. Mrs. Mulgrich had the jar in her hands and gave the length of the porch one final look before I heard a familiar "Humph" and then the slam of the door. Whew! That was a narrow escape. I sat there frozen for a minute or two.

I wanted to be sure that Mrs. Mulgrich and her annoying little counterpart were not coming back outside. Part of me couldn't blame the dog for being so angry. What self-respecting dog would ever want to be called Truffles? Then there was that moment that shocked me the most, when I heard tenderness in Mrs. Mulgrich's voice when she was talking to Truffles. Who would have thought it? Mrs. Mulgrich was capable of showing kindness. Maybe there was a glimmer of hope my plan would work after all.

I checked my watch – 6:57. I couldn't wait any longer. I slid out from under the bushes and ran as quickly as I could while watching for any holes in the ground. After making sure it was safe to cross, I sprinted from the road and into the safety of my grandma's kitchen. I quickly checked my watch – 6:59. "Mission Complete," I muttered breathlessly.

Grandma was sitting at the table waiting for my return. "Congratulations, soldier!" she exclaimed as she patted the chair where I normally sat. "Come, have a seat and tell me all about your mission." I sat down letting the leftover adrenaline run its course. I was starting to speak when Grandma interrupted. "Don't tell me you forgot about phase four, soldier?" I thought carefully. There was no fourth phase only three.

"What is the. . ." I began but was cut off again by Grandma.

"Operation Lima Beans!" she chortled as she pushed a steaming plate in my direction.

Two days passed, and the morning of the 15th arrived, bringing along with it The 23rd Annual Strawberry Shortcake Festival. I sat at the kitchen table with the fan turned, blowing directly on me. It was my feeble attempt to try and cool down from the stifling heat. Mornings seemed to take so long to pass when you were waiting to do something fun. The Strawberry Shortcake Festival was the biggest thing that happened in our town all year. We all gathered down at Whispering Willows Park and spent the day barbequing and taking part in the planned festivities. You could always count on a pie-eating contest. I am still trying to figure out why they even call it a contest because Bubba "Two-Bellies" McFinn always won. No one has even come close to his astounding 23 pies in 3 minutes. I turn green just watching him. My favorite was the three-legged race. I had never won, but I loved watching old Willy Jenkins. He had a peg leg and he insisted because he walked with a cane, that was considered three legs. Most everyone had good spirits about it. However, there were always a few who complained and rambled on about rules being broken. Someone once made the mistake of questioning him. Ol' Mr. Jenkins chased him down with his cane shouting words like "scallywag" and "hornswaggle." No one has ever questioned him again!

There were many other fun festivities planned, and while I was looking forward to going, my mind kept drifting to one thing, Mrs. Mulgrich. I was wondering if she was going to take me up on the invitation and come to the festival. After I carried out Operation Giving Jar two days ago, things seemed very uneventful at Mrs. Mulgrich's. I would normally see her out puttering around and her pooch running back and forth across her yard like a noisy little wind-up toy. But the last two days, I hadn't seen them at all.

Grandma came into the kitchen looking rather festive. She wore a red and white checked shirt and a long red skirt. On her shirt instead of regular round buttons, were little strawberry-shaped buttons. Her hair was pulled back into a neat bun and she had a strawberry clip pinned on each side of her hair. "Wow, Grandma, you look very . . . red!" I teased. I kept looking out the window over to Mrs. Mulgrich's. I glanced over at Grandma while she prepared the blackberry lemonade to take to the picnic. I noticed one important piece of her outfit than I had missed earlier. Pinned right above her shirt pocket was her angel pin. The sunlight bounced off of it giving it a glowing appearance.

"What has you so distracted today, Billy? Normally you are much more excited about the festival. Are you feeling ill?" Grandma asked concerned.

"No, Grandma, I'm fine. I guess I just have alot on my mind," I muttered as I turned to look out the window.

"Oh, I see!" Grandma exclaimed. "You are looking to see if Mrs. Mulrgich is going to come to the festival." I was now turned facing the window crooking my head to try and get a better view. Grandma walked over behind me and placed her hands on my shoulders. "Billy, whether she comes or not, I am very proud of you. What you did the other day was wonderful."

"I know, Grandma, it's just. . ." I lost my concentration when I saw a strange car pull in Mrs. Mulgrich's driveway and saw Mrs. Mulgrich leave her house and get into the front seat of the car.

"Well, I'll be!" Grandma muttered under her breath and went to finish preparing for the picnic. My mind was racing with the possibilities. Could Mrs. Mulgrich be going to the festival? I didn't want to get my hopes up. After all, there were a number of different things she could be doing. Perhaps she found someone with a similar culinary interest and they were attending a seminar on 101 ways to cook children. I could hardly wait for 2:00 to arrive to see if Mrs. Mulgrich would be at the picnic and who this person was driving the mysterious car.

There was only a couple hours left before the picnic and lots to do to get ready. So I decided the time would pass much faster if I pitched in and helped. While Grandma added the last ingredients into her potato salad, I gathered all the contents for our picnic basket. Most everything was complete inside so I headed outdoors. Boy, was it hot! Days like this I loved to go and spend the day at the old swimming hole at Big Gully Creek. Maybe after the festival I could convince Grandma to let me go and cool off.

But for now, there was work to be done. Grandma's gardens seemed to be calling out for a drink. I headed over to the garden hose and turned it on. I let the water run for a few seconds to flush out the warm water and took a drink of the refreshing cool water. After watering all of the gardens and taking a quick walk to my favorite meadow, it was time to leave for the picnic!

I quickly helped Grandma load the car and we left for Whispering Willows Park. All through the town there were signs with arrows pointing to the park and saying things like "Join Us Toady for Springcreek's 23rd Annual Strawberry Shortcake Festival, All Are Welcome!" We arrived at 2:00 on the dot and the park was already bustling with action. There was a huge white banner that spread across the length of the pavilion. Written in large red lettering it read, "Welcome To The Home of the World's Best Strawberry Shortcake!"

There was a group of men gathered around the charcoal grills preparing them for their long day of barbecuing. There was a gathering of women under the pavilion laying out different dishes to be shared by all.

Old Mayor Ackerman was fashioned in his bathing suit, sitting in the dunk tank wearing a rather worried look on his face. There were children of all ages everywhere to be seen. Some playing tag, others swinging. Some of the older girls were just walking around in groups talking. Like they were too mature to run around and play. I'll never understand girls!

While I unloaded Grandma's car, I examined the parking lot for the strange car I had seen earlier. Nothing! I still had hope, though. Maybe whoever it was just dropped off Mrs. Mulgrich at the picnic and left.

I spent the first 20 minutes scouring the park looking for Mrs. Mulgrich. I got my hopes up at one point. There was a lady who looked just like her from the back, but when she turned around, it was just old Mrs. Kleever, the neighborhood seamstress. I dragged myself over to where the food was set up and found a huge fudge brownie to drown my sorrows in.

Feeling a little better after the brownie, they announced the water balloon toss was about to begin! Looking forward to getting hit with a few water balloons to cool myself down, I hurried over to where the crowd of children was forming. What happened next completely took me by surprise. While I was waiting for the toss to begin, there was some sort of commotion and the next thing I knew water balloons were flying everywhere! Not wanting to get left out of the action, I grabbed an arsenal of water balloons and started launching them into the crowd of children. I had one balloon left, and I was aiming to hit my best friend Johnny who was quite a distance from me. I launched the water balloon as far as I could. I couldn't tell if I hit my intended target because a crowd of kids ran in front of me just as I released the balloon. The balloon war stopped abruptly and there was an eerie silence that spread throughout the whole park and the only thing to be heard was hushed gasps.

I frantically looked around trying to see what it was that had happened. I spotted Grandma under the pavilion with her head hung down, hand covering her eyes while she shook her head from side to side in disbelief.

Whatever it was that had just happened could not be good! When the mob finally cleared, I discovered what it was that was causing this sudden change in the atmosphere. When I saw what had happened, I wanted to find myself a giant hole and bury myself alive! Standing about 25 feet in front of me were three people, two of whom I had never seen before. There was a very tall gentleman holding a bushel basket with a very amused look on his face. Standing next to him was a girl who appeared to be about my age or maybe a little younger. She had big brown eyes and long, curly brown hair that was pulled up into a ponytail. She was covering her face with her hand trying to disguise her fits of laughter. Standing in front of them was a very wet Mrs. Mulgrich. My renegade water balloon must have found its way to her and exploded on contact.

With nowhere to run, I stood there awaiting my impending doom. What Mrs. Mulgrich did next took everyone at Whispering Willows Park by surprise. Her face scrunched up like an old prune, started to soften. Then Mrs. Mulgrich did something I have never seen before. . . she smiled!

I was frozen in shock at her response. Normally she would have a conniption fit if my bicycle came within a foot of her yard, but today a water balloon exploded on her and she smiled! All of our eyes were still on Mrs. Mulgrich as she walked toward me, her smile widening. Wait a minute. . . was this a happy smile on her face or a menacing smile, one of those smiles that someone flashes before doing something evil. Well, if she ate me now at least there would be witnesses. Before I could even see it coming, something hit my chest and I felt warm water saturating my shirt. Mrs. Mulgrich stood right in front of me with a satisfied look on her face.

"Ah, Billy. Don't take it personally," she teased. "What's good for the goose is good for the gander, right?" I just smiled and nodded my head, still in utter disbelief at her unexpected response. Everyone's eyes were on Mrs. Mulgrich as she turned away from me and entered the safety of the pavilion. As soon as she was under cover, she yelled out to the brown-eyed girl who she came with, "Come on, Becky, show them what you got!"

The next few minutes were a blur - just lots of water balloons whizzing by me in every direction. In between trying to dodge incoming water missiles, I was able to observe a few things. I was quite impressed with Mrs. Mulgrich's young friend. For a girl, she had a pretty mean arm! But what I remember the most from those few moments was glancing over at Mrs. Mulgrich, seeing her laughing and enjoying the sight in front of her.

After things had finally settled down from the balloon battle, I noticed there was some more excitement starting. I hurried over to the group of children not wanting to miss out on any of the action. The tall gentleman, who had arrived with Mrs. Mulgrich, was in the center of the mob with the bushel basket that he had been carrying sitting next to him. A sign was fixed to the basket that read "Mrs. Mulgrich's Lost and Found." Inside the basket there was

an assortment of unfortunate items that had found themselves in Mrs. Mulgrich's yard over the years. There were balls of all varieties, baseballs, footballs, and kick balls, to name a few. I spotted a cap gun and some yo-yos in the mix.

There were even a few GI Joe figures I was hoping no one would claim. A line started to form as one by one children looked through the basket to reclaim their lost treasure. When it got to be my turn, I dove into the basket looking for my long-lost baseball. I searched for a couple of minutes with no luck. Finally when I just about reached the bottom, I found my ball. It was just as I remembered. The stitching on one side was coming loose and written in red marker was "Property of Billy Newman." Thrilled to be reunited with my baseball, I went off to find Johnny to see if he was up for a game of catch.

The rest of the afternoon went by rather quickly. Johnny and I won the scavenger hunt, although some of the older ladies did not appreciate our choice for something brown. They threw themselves quite a stink. Really, I don't know what the fuss was all about. It was just a harmless garter snake. It was all worth it in the end though.

Johnny and I both won our very own box of Bazooka Bubblegum! Bubba "Two-Bellies" beat his record and finished off 25 pies in 3 minutes. I was a little worried about him after the contest. He spent most of the afternoon running back and forth to the men's room. As usual, Old Willy Jenkins took home the first-place ribbon for the three-legged race. Boy, did he put on quite a show this year! As he crossed the finish line, he let out a huge cackle and just kept on going. With the finish line still attached and trailing behind him, he hobbled along hooting and hollering with his hands and cane flying wildly above his head. He never stopped. He just kept on running and running until

he disappeared into the forest. The only trace left of him was his mad ramblings that were fading in the distance. Deputy Lynch had to go after him and bring him back. I think if he hadn't, that crazy old cur-mudgeon would have just kept on going!

While I was filling up on my third hot dog and second helping of Grandma's potato salad, I noticed my picnic table was right next to Mrs. Mulgrich's. She seemed to be enjoying the company of the ladies who sat around her. At one point, she broke out in a fit of laughter. She raised her hands to her mouth to try and stifle the noise that was pouring uncontrollably out of her. If I didn't hear it myself, I would have never believed it but Mrs. Mulgrich actually snorted! Just to set the record straight, these were not quiet lady-like snorts. We are talking about snorts of earth-shaking proportions! I was quite entertained watching Mrs. Mulgrich. This was not the same spiteful old lady I had known just a few days ago. Today Mrs. Mulgrich was positively glowing! She began waving her hands in front of her face to try and fan herself and catch a breath or two when I noticed it. On Mrs. Mulgrich's right hand she was wearing the silver ring with the flowers on it! At that moment I was on cloud nine!

I started to recall what Grandma had said the other day. Something about planting kind seeds and I would reap some sort of harvest. I am not sure what she meant by that. But what I did know was my heart was so full of joy and love right now it felt as if it could burst.

My thoughts were interrupted by something I overheard. I know it is extremely rude to eavesdrop, but my curiosity won the battle and I did it anyway! Mrs. Mulgrich began explaining to her friends who the two strangers were that accompanied her here. It turns out Mrs. Mulgrich did have family after all. The tall gentleman was her son Merritt and that Becky girl was her 10-year-old granddaughter. It seems that there was some sort of falling out between Merritt and Mrs. Mulgrich many years ago.

She explained that the last time she had seen Becky, she was no more than a few months old. She went around the table passing out apologies to the women for the hurtful things she had done. Her voice was starting to crack and her eyes moistened as she asked for their forgiveness. She described how she allowed bitterness to harden her heart. Tears were flowing down her face, and the women gathered around to comfort her.

After a few moments Mrs. Mulgrich composed herself. "I know what I am about to say is going to sound crazy," Mrs. Mulgrich said softly. "But an angel paid me a visit the other day. I cannot explain what happened to my heart that day, but every ounce of bitterness melted away. The first thing I did was call my son and begged for his forgiveness. Then I decided I had wasted the past 10 years wallowing in misery. But somehow I was pulled out of my sinking pit and every breath that is left in me will be spent in joy."

I couldn't stop a huge smile from spreading across my whole face. I overheard the other women asking her for certain details of this visit with this "angel". But Mrs. Mulgrich would just smile and tenderly reply, "I am sorry. That is private."

I was so completely overwhelmed with pure bliss that I did not hear Johnny. When I came to he was waving his hands in front of my face. "Whoo Hoo! Are you there, Billy? Come on, it's time for kickball!" He exclaimed as he pulled me off the bench.

Thankfully, after the picnic Grandma let Johnny and me go cool off down at the swimming hole. I was the first one to the rope swing that was tied to the mammoth willow tree that shaded the pond. I swung back and forth a few times letting my toes skim the top of the water before I finally let go. The cool water felt like heaven. I didn't really feel like playing. The day and the heat had left me exhausted. Thankfully, Johnny was worn out from the picnic as well. We lazily floated on our backs enjoying the quiet.

I drifted effortlessly across the water. Memories of the day rolled through my head forming an effortless smile across my face. . I think I finally understood what Grandma was trying to say. That by some miracle, by giving kindness we cannot help but feel it ourselves. Talk about a win/win situation! I never in my whole life felt the exhilaration I felt today! My head was literally spinning with all of today's events whirling around my mind. I tried to empty my head, but as hard as I tried, there was one thought that kept finding its way back in. It was that girl Becky, Mrs. Mulgrich's granddaughter with the big brown eyes and the mean right arm.

A few years had passed since my very first Operation Giving Jar mission with Mrs.. Mulgrich. To this very day, Mrs. Mulgrich still had no idea that I was the one behind the mysterious appearance of the jar on her doorstep. Her granddaughter Becky came over every weekend and spent almost the whole summer with her. Over the past few years, Becky and I had become pretty good friends. I never would have guessed there was a girl out there who enjoyed fishing as much as me! Even though I don't like keeping secrets from my friends, I would never tell Becky I was the one who placed The Giving Jar on her grandma's front porch. Mrs. Mulgrich stayed true to her word and did not let bitterness rule her life anymore. Her yard actually became a place where kids from the neighborhood went and played.

There always seemed to be a group of kids congregating on her lawn. I think it may have had something to do with the homemade chocolate chip cookies she would always have on hand!

Oh, and about that ridiculous rumor of her eating children - not true! Would you believe I found out she doesn't even eat meat. She is a vegetarian! I was never worried, anyway. In fact, she thinks that fruits and vegetables are so important, she goes to different families, especially ones that have lots of children, and delivers fresh produce. Mostly bananas, which has earned her the new nickname – "The Banana Lady"! In my opinion, that is a huge step up from "Child-Eater"!

Mrs. Mulgrich's dog, Truffles, had even seemed to turn over a new leaf. Instead of yelping at me all of the time, she actually let's me pick her up. She does tend to slobber all over my face with her wet kisses. That's okay with me though! I am willing to take her stinky dog breath, any day of the week, over that ear-piercing bark!

Over the past few years, Grandma has sent me on many more top secret missions. For me, nothing was more exciting than when Grandma announced it was a time for another Operation Giving Jar to be executed. Never once did I go on a mission without wearing Grandpa's coat. Grandma and I both thought it brought me good luck. There have been a few close calls, but I was never discovered when in the line of duty. Grandma and I often talk and laugh about that day I tried to confiscate the jar and stuff it full of worms.

I have often wondered how that jar ended up on Grandma's doorstep and who could have placed it there. One day while out on the front porch, Grandma in her rocking chair and I sprawled across the floor, I decided to ask Grandma about the appearance of the jar. She sat quiet for a moment or two looking very thoughtful. "Come with me, Billy," she said as she rose from her rocking chair. I followed her over to the porch's edge and she began to point at something. "What does that look like to you?" She asked while she motioned toward the tree that held the swing.

"It's a willow tree, Grandma!" I replied as I gazed at the tree and the amazing sunset that decorated the sky behind it.

"Just a willow tree?" Grandma questioned once again.

Confused, I responded, "Umm yup, Grandma. I am pretty sure that is just a willow tree." Grandma turned and stared out at the tree as if she were studying it.

"Well, I disagree with you, Billy." She said in a very factual tone, never taking her eyes from the tree. "When I look out at the tree, I see many different things. I see something that helps make the air that you and I breathe. And what about the robins that build their nests in the tree every year they return? That is not just a tree to them. . .that is their home. And what about you, Billy, did you forget?" She asked as she turned to face me. "Look very closely," she continued as she pointed at the tree again. "When you were younger, that wasn't just a tree. One day it was your magic fortress, a place where you would battle fire-breathing dragons. Another day it was your pirate ship that you were sailing to discover some long-lost buried treasure."

Wow! How could I have forgotten that, I thought as I looked out at the tree as if it were my long-lost friend.

I felt Grandma reach for my hand as she started to speak once again. "That is my point, Billy. Things are not always what they appear to be." Now holding both of my hands in hers she continued. "Your hands Billy, are they just hands?"

"Ehh - I guess not," I answered somewhat unsure of myself.

"Right!" Grandma exclaimed. "These here," she said as she shook my hands, "are two angels." I looked at Grandma, with obvious surprise on my face. I was expecting something along the lines of back-scratchers, certainly nothing with wings!

"Angels?" I asked looking confusedly at my hands.

"Yes Billy," Grandma replied, "They are angels. A pair of ordinary hands, just like yours, can carry out the work of an angel. Every time you went on a mission or did something thoughtful for others, through your hands kindness flowed, touching people's lives in the most unimaginable ways. Out of kindness and love, miracles can happen, Billy."

Grandma finished speaking and moved back to her rocking chair. I turned around to face her. I was mulling over what Grandma had just said when my thoughts were broken by the sound of her voice. "So, Billy, back to the question you had asked me earlier. . ."

Grandma couldn't finish her sentence when I interrupted her with, "Yes! Who do you think put the jar on your doorstep, Grandma?"

Rocking back and forth in her rocking chair, she gazed over at me with a smile spreading across her face and replied, "An angel."

Time has an amazing way of passing us by. It seems it was just yesterday I was a boy and enjoying the summers down at Big Gully Creek catching trout and spending lazy afternoons down at the old swimming hole with Johnny.  But it wasn't yesterday. In fact, almost 20 years had passed since then and here I was married with two children of my own, a beautiful wife, and a house in which to raise my family.

The sun filtering through the curtains acted as my alarm clock, and I rose before anyone else in the house. I peeked outside to see if the weather man was right. I had a to-do list that was growing by the second, and he promised today was going to be the perfect day for working outside. Checking the sky, I could not find one cloud in sight. That was promising.  I glanced down at my lawn that needed to be cleaned and couldn't believe my eyes. It seemed too early in the year, but hopping across the lawn was a robin with its breakfast wiggling in its beak.

I was taken back to when I was younger and Grandma's silly tradition of running around the yard beating pots and pans when the first robin of spring was spotted. For a moment, I considered waking my children, running down to the kitchen, and raiding the cupboards for the pots and pans. Part of me felt bad for breaking this tradition over the years, but it always seemed to happen on a day there was too much to do. Besides what would our neighbors think? Oh look, Mom, there they are. . . the Newmans doing their annual rain dance. So it was decided then, spring would have to make its entrance without the pots and pans parade.

I quickly dressed and headed down the stairs and for the front door to get an early start on my list. Right before I made it to the door the phone began to ring. For goodness sakes, it was only 7:30 in the morning, and our phone was  already ringing off the hook! I quickly dashed to the phone so it would not wake the rest of the house. I was surprised to hear my cousin Sarah's voice when I answered the phone. However, my shock quickly turned to sadness when Sarah gave me the news of Grandma. She had been quite sick these past few years, and at some point during the night she had passed away.

After I hung up with Sarah, I went to the living room and sunk into the couch. I did something I had not done in a very long time - I cried. My grandma was my whole world growing up. As I grew older and went off to college I had to live quite a distance from Grandma. We still talked all the time, but it wasn't the same as being able to wrap my arms around her and give her a hug. Then it came time to find a job. That took me even farther away from where I grew up. It seemed as the years passed we talked less and less. Not because my love for her faded, but always because I felt I was always too busy. With tears rolling down my face and guilt ripping me apart at the seams, I sobbed myself to sleep.

I woke a couple hours later to my daughter Cassie tapping my shoulder and asking if I was okay. It was very unusual for me to sleep in so late, it must have slightly alarmed her to find me conked out on the couch at almost 10:30 in the morning. I smiled and wished her a huge good morning and sprung off the couch, picked her up, and whirled her around in the air. Over the years it seems I had not been as playful with my children as I should have either. Cassie shot me a strange look when I set her down and murmured something about me having a fever and going to get her mom. I told her while she was getting Mom to be sure and get her brother Henry, whom we named after my grandfather, and come back to the living room.

While Cassie was off looking for her mother and Henry, I had decided I was going to spend all of today with my family. My children didn't get much of an opportunity to know Grandma very well. I felt terrible for not taking them to see her more often.  Right now, memories were all that I had to offer them and I intended to share every last one I had. Maybe I would take the next week off from work.  We could spend some time in Springcreek. We could stay at the old house, and I could take them fishing down at Big Gully Creek and show them all the places Grandma and I used to go and things we used to do. Besides, they had another great grandma who lived there that they didn't get to see enough of either.

Cassie returned with Henry and their mother, and I asked for them all to have a seat. I explained to them Great Grandma had passed away and although they didn't know her very well she loved them very much. We sat in the living room the next few hours talking and sharing stories. Since I'd spent the most time with Grandma, I was the one talking the most. I would have to stop every few minutes to answer a question or wait until their laughter was under control. They were amazed by the stories.

Their favorite ones seemed to be ones that involved some form of embarrassment to me. For instance on my 18th birthday, Grandma posted pictures all around town saying, "If you happen to see Billy today, wish him a Happy 18th Birthday." That doesn't sound so bad, does it? Well, it would have been fine but the picture she chose was when I was about two and I was going through a nose-picking stage. I tried to deny it and say it must be another Billy, but our town was too small and there was only one Billy turning 18 that year in the whole town.  And as luck would have it, it was me, good old nose-picking Billy. It took forever for people to let that one go!

They also loved to hear the story about the day their mother and I met and how I hit their Great Grandma Mulgrich with a water balloon. They wanted to hear that story a few times.  I told them the tradition of the first robin of spring, and suddenly I remembered what I had seen this morning through my window. Cassie and Henry were thrilled to find out I had seen the robin and couldn't wait to go ring in spring properly. Becky was a little worried about the neighbors, but after a second of thinking about it she decided to join in, too.

We all raced to the kitchen to find proper ceremonial pots and pans when we were interrupted by the doorbell ringing.  Henry and Cassie were trying different pots on their heads, giggling at the sight of each other and Becky was looking for wooden spoons, so I ran to answer the door.

When I opened the door, no one was there. No more than 30 seconds could have passed from the time the doorbell sounded, but whoever it was left already. I walked out on the porch and called "Hello" just to make sure no one was there, but there was no one. It was when I turned to walk back into the house that I was frozen by what I saw. Sitting on my doorstep was a jar, not just any jar but the jar that sat on my grandma's kitchen table for all those years.

I couldn't move for a few minutes. I just stood there staring at the jar wondering if it were some sort of mirage that was going to disappear the second I try and pick it up. I moved slowly toward the jar still anticipating it would vanish into thin air, but it did no such thing. I picked the jar up and held it in my hand and allowed my emotions to wash over me.

After a few minutes, I returned into the house with the jar and heard all the excitement that was in the kitchen moving closer toward me. "I could only find three wooden spoons," I heard Becky say as they all appeared from the hallway. From the looks on their faces, I must have been a sight to see. The children just stood there gaping at me with confusion mixed with a little fear. Cassie dropped her pan and ran toward me crying, "See, mom, I told you he was sick!"

I must have looked sick, my face swollen and my eyes red and puffy all while I was holding this jar in my arms like it were a newborn baby. I took Cassie in my arms and assured her I was not sick at all. In fact it was quite the opposite. I was incredibly fine. I held out the jar and showed everyone what it was that I was holding in my hands. Becky gasped as she recognized the jar. She, too, saw it sit on Grandma's table for many years.

However, now as I held it, it contained more than just that tattered note that I had read on Grandma's porch so long ago. Cassie and Henry wore a puzzled expression and didn't know what to make of this jar in my hands. "Daddy, who was at the door?" Henry asked still wearing a pot on his head.

I glanced down at the jar and then to my family who I cherished so much and answered, "An angel."

I headed back to the kitchen with my family following close behind. I asked everyone to have a seat at the table and set the jar down for everyone to see. I had left one story out earlier when I was sharing my memories of Grandma. Now was the time to reveal the story of The Giving Jar to my family. I told them about the day I had tried to sneak it off the kitchen table and got caught and the afternoon I spent out on the porch with Grandma learning about her Giving Jar and my grandpa. I told them all about our secret Giving Jar missions, but not once did I mention who we delivered the jars to. At one point during the conversation, Becky interrupted me and began to say something about her grandma. She quickly quieted and would not repeat what it was that she had said. She just listened to the rest of the story with a knowing smile creeping across her face.

Henry was fascinated by stories of his great grandpa and wore a proud smile on his face when he had heard he descended from a war hero. Cassie was interested in the stories as well, but I noticed her gaze kept drifting back to the jar sitting on the table.

"Sooo. . . This is Great Grandma's jar?" Cassie asked eyes full of wonder.

"I think so, but let's open it to see for sure," I replied as I took the jar in my hands and began to turn the lid. Cassie and Henry sat as still as statues, their eyes as big and round as silver dollars. Even Becky's eyes sparkled with hints of magic and awe. I twisted the lid off the jar and was overtaken by the scent that poured from the jar. As I breathed in the sweet fragrance, it sent me spiraling back into my distant past. It was the aroma of Grandma's yard and her many gardens. Somehow that distinct smell made its way into the jar and now lingered throughout my kitchen.

I reached inside and pulled out the note. It had aged quite a bit since that day I read it on Grandma's porch. I was almost afraid to open and read it for fear it would crumble in my hands. I delicately opened the fragile note and read it out loud for all of my family to hear. I could barely make out any of the words and had I not written dozens of these note when I was growing up, I would not have been able to make out the writing at all. I stood with the note in my hands and looked to my children to find they hadn't moved an inch and their eyes fixed to the note in my hands.

Cassie reached into the jar next. I heard her gasp when I caught a glimpse of what she had taken from The Giving Jar. It left me speechless. In her hand, she held a silver angel pin and the tip of the left wing was tarnished. I was positive this was Grandma's angel pin she had worn for all those years. Time was kind to this small brooch. It was just as brilliant as the first day I saw it.

"Grandma's?" Henry whispered as he gently traced the left wing of the angel, still resting in the palm of his sister's hand. All I could manage was a slight nod of the head to confirm his suspicions were correct. It seems that the appearance of the pin left everyone else in the room wordless as well. Silence filled the air and intertwined with the pleasant scent that still mingled about. Henry moved suddenly and reached for the jar, bringing all of us back to reality with him.

He reached in and pulled out something wrapped in tissue paper. "A present?" Henry wondered excitedly as he ripped the tissue apart to reveal what lie hidden inside. A roar of laughter broke out amongst all of us when we saw a very disappointed Henry holding a broken wooden spoon. This wasn't just any wooden spoon, though. This was the official wooden spoon I had used to welcome in past springs with. In fact, it got so much use, one year while parading around Grandma's lawn, it broke right in half! Grandma and I both agreed there was still a lot of life left in the spoon, so we saved the bottom half and used it for many more years.

Cassie jumped up from her chair. "This is good news!" She cried while pointing at the spoon in Henry's hands. Henry did not share in her enthusiasm and kept looking down at the spoon as if it were going to transform into something much more exciting.

"We have four now!" Cassie called out as she scooped up the three wooden spoons that lay by her mother and began to pass one out to each of us. She gave Henry a new wooden spoon and held her hand out for the broken one. He gladly swapped with his sister, and seemed a little surprised she would want it. Cassie walked over to me with two wooden spoons in her hands. When she stood before me she held out the broken wooden spoon. "I think that Grandma would like it if you took this one," she said as she placed the half of spoon in my hands. "It was yours, wasn't it, Daddy?" She asked as she watched me examine my old spoon.

"Yes, Cassie, it was." I replied. I stood there in amazement for a moment not by the jar or the spoon but by the love that washed over me that I had for my family.

"What are we waiting for?" Henry cried out as he passed out all the pans and adjusted the pot on his head. I looked to Becky, who was already sporting a pot on her head and armed with a wooden spoon and pan.

"Are you ready, Mrs. Newman?" I teased as I picked up my pan.

She placed a bright red pot on my head and replied, "Well, what are we waiting for, Mr. Newman? Let's go welcome spring in properly!"

Becky and I quietly stood near the edge of their beds after tucking in Henry and Cassie for the night. They were exhausted from the long day's events and were asleep before their heads even touched the pillow. We spent a few minutes just watching, as they drifted further into their slumber. So peaceful they looked as they traveled deeper into the magical corners of their minds, to the place where dreams come to life. In the stillness of those next few minutes, I just closed my eyes, thankful for this wonderful day. I was saddened to know that Grandma was no longer here with us in a physical sense. I would miss her smile and her gentle way. But somehow, as I stood here with my cherished family I felt Grandma's presence all around us.

"Billy, are you okay?" Becky asked in a hushed voice as she brushed her hand across the top of mine.

I gazed over to Cassie and Henry and replied, "I am much more than okay." I inched closer to where they lay and tenderly placed a kiss atop each of their heads. I turned around to find Becky yawning and trying not to surrender to sleep herself. "You need your rest, too, Becky," I whispered as we treaded across the bedroom floor and quietly closed the door behind us. We crossed the hall and entered our room. "I just have a few things I need to take care of before I turn in for the night," I said softly as I brushed a stray piece of hair from Becky's face. She collapsed onto the bed and started to mumble something about the jar and her Grandma Mulgrich as I covered her with the blankets. I couldn't quite make out what she was saying and soon her words softly faded into a quiet snore.

Silently, I closed the bedroom door and headed down the stairs. I felt a cool breeze drifting up the staircase coming from the kitchen. We must have left a window open from earlier today. It turned out the weatherman was right. Today had been beautiful. Just the sort of day that is perfect for losing that nagging list of things to do. Walking through the kitchen, I caught a glimpse of the white moon that hung suspended in the sky. The curtains billowed from the chilled nighttime breeze.

I rested against the window sill for a few moments letting the gusts of brisk air clear my tired mind. I was trying to sort out the mixture of conflicting emotions that were coursing through my body. I felt grief and sorrow for the loss of my Grandma, yet pure joy and happiness for having been blessed with the time I had with her. One thing was certain, I was a much better person for the time I had been graciously given to spend with her. I reached up and closed the window, causing the curtains to fall limp against the windowpane. I gazed out the window up into the black sky and stood in awe at the majesty of the night. It was as if the sky were a dark canvas and the pale moon the artist's palette, and millions of specks of illuminating white paint were the stars that decorated the canvas adding just the right touch. It was truly nature's masterpiece.

As I slowly drifted back to my surroundings, a tiny reflection in the windowpane caught my attention. It was the jar. I turned around to find the jar on the kitchen table, right where we had left it earlier. The moon shone through the window behind me sending beams of soft light across the room onto the table. The moonlight cast off the swaying tree branches and filtered across the room in the most amazing patterns.

As I looked over at the jar, I could feel guilt starting to tear away at me. This jar, The Giving Jar, was such an important part of my childhood. How could have I let that part of my life slip away? I crossed the kitchen to where the jar stood and gradually my guilt was exchanged for a new emotion, excitement. I knew what I had to do. I was reunited not just with the jar, but with the whole tradition that went along with it.

I carefully picked up the note, gently placed it back into jar, and twisted the lid back on. I gently slid Grandma's angel pin across the table until it lay in front of Cassie's chair. I quickly turned from the table and rushed out of the room to the hallway closet. I threw open the closet door and began to search. I knew what I needed was buried in here somewhere amongst my years of collecting. There was the mushroom farm in a box I had to have. A pile of knit sweaters Becky's Aunt Edith knits for me. I get one for every Christmas, and I have to keep them handy in case she shows up for a surprise visit.

At last I found it; buried way over in the corner, peeking out behind file boxes was a green strap. I carefully pulled it to try to avoid the whole contents of the closet from spilling out on me. Success! I hurriedly unzipped the green canvas bag that Grandma had passed down to me all those years ago. I could smell the leather before the bag was fully unzipped. I pulled out Grandpa's jacket and let the bag fall to the floor. It had been years since I'd worn this coat, I wondered if it would still fit.

I pulled my arms through the sleeves and was surprised to find I could even zip it up. I walked over to the mirror and examined myself in my Grandpa's coat. The first thing I noticed was the wings. It was still in the same spot where Grandma had pinned it on when I was about Henry's age. I ran my fingers across the wings and memories of my grandma and our many missions flooded my thoughts, bringing a smile to my face. Finally, I thought as I placed my hands inside the coat pockets, Grandma has gotten what she had been longing for since the day Grandpa left for the war. They were together once again.

That was odd. I felt something in my pocket. I must have left something in there on one of my last missions. I pulled out what appeared to be a folded-up envelope. I unfolded it and had to prop myself against the wall when I saw the writing.  In blue ink was my name "Billy" written in my grandma's handwriting. Trembling I opened the envelope to find a note and a key. The key was attached to a pewter keychain that appeared to be a bouquet of flowers. I noticed on the back there was an inscription. Written in tiny letters, it read: "Never forget your roots, Come home often." This must be a house key to Grandma's place, but how? She must have placed the envelope in there when I was packing to go off to college.

I unfolded the note that was written on just a plain white piece of paper. Somehow it held that distinct scent, the same aroma that had poured from the jar earlier that day. It was the fragrance of Grandma and her many gardens. I took a deep breath, inhaling the sweet smell, and began to read. . .

*My Dearest Billy,*

*How lucky I have been to be your Grandma. I want you to know there is a part of my heart*
*that belongs only to you. So now when we are apart, I will never be lonely. I will carry you*
*with me at all times in that part of my  heart only you can fill.*


My eyes were filling with tears making it impossible to read. I gave myself a moment to dry my eyes and continued.


*Billy, you were a wonderful child so curious and always so full of hope. You have grown into*
*a fine young man just like I always knew you would. Just make me a promise, Billy.*
*Hold onto the part of yourself and live every day in that sweet child-like wonder.*
*May your clouds never just be clouds!*


*Love With All My Heart,*
*Grandma*


I pulled the paper to my chest, and my tears turned into sobs of a little boy

I promised Grandma even though I had once I would never lose that part of myself again. I folded the note back up and put it in the envelope with the key and slid it into my jeans pocket. I gathered up Grandpa's bag and returned to the kitchen, stopping along the way to the pantry.

Once back in the kitchen, I took off Grandpa's coat and placed it back in the green sack. I zipped up the bag, and at that moment I knew it was no longer just mine and Grandpa's coat. At the foot of Henry's kitchen table chair, I placed the bag. I examined the table carefully. In the center sat Grandma's Giving Jar with the aged note folded into a square. Grandma's angel pin lay waiting in front of Cassie's chair, and Grandpa's coat waited for Henry next to his chair hidden in the bag.

There was only one thing missing. Sitting on the kitchen counter was what I had retrieved from the pantry just a few moments ago. I removed the empty glass jar from the counter and positioned it right next to Grandma's.

Exhausted, I headed towards the stairs. When I reached the bottom of the staircase I turned to glance at the kitchen table and all it held. Overcome with emotion, I continued up the stairs, knowing everything was in its perfect place for tomorrow morning and Cassie and Henry's very first Operation Giving Jar.

My Dearest Billy

How lucky I have been to be your Grandma. I want you to know there is a part of my heart that belongs only to you, so now when we are apart, I will never be lonely I will carry you with me at all times in that part of my heart only you can fill.

Billy you were a wonderful child so curious and always so full of hope. You have grown into a fine young man just like I always knew you would. You make me a promise. Billy hold onto the part of yourself and live every day in that sweet child-like wonder.

May your clouds Never just be Clouds.

Love With All My Heart,
Grandma

# The Story Behind "The Giving Jar"
## - A special message from author Krissy Smith

It is with great pleasure that I am able to share "The Giving Jar" with you. This book has very special meaning to me, as it is based on a tradition that my young family has grown to love. I am very passionate about living my life with a giving spirit and often encourage my children to do the same. The call to give dwells deep within my heart, and looks for every opportunity to present itself in a healthy, productive way.

One afternoon, my husband and I had heard of a family that was having a difficult time making ends meet. It just so happened at that time, we had been blessed with a little extra money. We decided that it was in our hearts, to pass our blessing on to this family in need. We considered many different methods of giving the money to the family, but we struggled to find the right way. There was one challenge that we could not seem to overcome. We wanted to be sure they received the money, but at the same time, we did not want our identities revealed. . . Hence "The Giving Jar" was born.

We prepared the jar with the money and added a special note of encouragement. My husband who had been in the Army, instructed our three older children about the mission that lay ahead of them and what was expected of them. He went on to ask them if they accepted the mission. The looks on their faces were priceless. They were bubbling over with excitement and anticipation as they accepted the mission and the tasks it included. They returned from their very first "Operation Giving Jar" exhilarated from the joy that giving brings, and filled with the overall thrill of the adventure. That moment, seeing my children so blissful to give to others, is a memory that I will cherish forever.

When one mission would come to a close, my children would anxiously await the orders for their next Giving Jar adventure. When our children had sleepovers, their guests would request if they too, could go on a giving mission. Of course, before they could participate my children insisted they take an oath of secrecy, to promise they would tell absolutely no one of their mission.

After many missions with my children and noticing how the act of giving had left such a mark on them, I decided it was time to share this story. . . our tradition, with others. For months, different ideas on how to present the story came and went, but not one of them resonated with me - That was until Billy.

He showed up in my head one night, at 2:30 am. He began to tell me all about himself and his journey with The Giving Jar. I pleaded with him to go away and come back in the morning! However, he proved to be very stubborn and insisted on talking to me right then and there! So it went from that point forward, most times in the middle of the night that Billy would come to visit me, and continue telling me his story. Although he did not keep the most convenient of schedules, I truly appreciated his visits and the story he had to tell of his time with The Giving Jar.

So now, as Billy's chapters come to a close, I turn the rest of the story, this life-long journey, over to you. I truly hope that "The Giving Jar" has touched your heart and inspired you to live your days with a giving spirit!